KT-503-226

This
Treasure Cove Story
belongs to

_____

SPIDER-MAN
NIGHT OF THE VULTURE!

A CENTUM BOOK 978-1-912396-36-8
Published in Great Britain by Centum Books Ltd.
This edition published 2018.

3 5 7 9 10 8 6 4 2

© 2018 MARVEL. marvelHQ.com

No part of this publication may be reproduced, stored in a retrieval
system, or transmitted in any form or by any means, electronic,
mechanical, photocopying, recording or otherwise without
the prior permission of the publishers.

Centum Books Ltd, 20 Devon Square, Newton Abbot,
Devon, TQ12 2HR, UK.

www.centumbooksltd.co.uk | books@centumbooksltd.co.uk
CENTUM BOOKS Limited Reg.No. 07641486.

A CIP catalogue record for this book is available
from the British Library.

Printed in China.

A Treasure Cove Story

MARVEL
SPIDER-MAN

Night of the Vulture!

By Frank J Berrios
Illustrated by Francesco Legramandi
and Silvano Scolari

As the news of an unusual crime spree spread across the city, the web-slinging hero known as Spider-Man took to the rooftops.

This doesn't make sense, thought Spider-Man. Several tech factories were broken into, all in one night. Who could be behind this? I'd better get to the scene of the crime.

'No clues here,' he mumbled as he swung away from the scene of the first robbery. 'Maybe I'll have better luck at those other places uptown.'

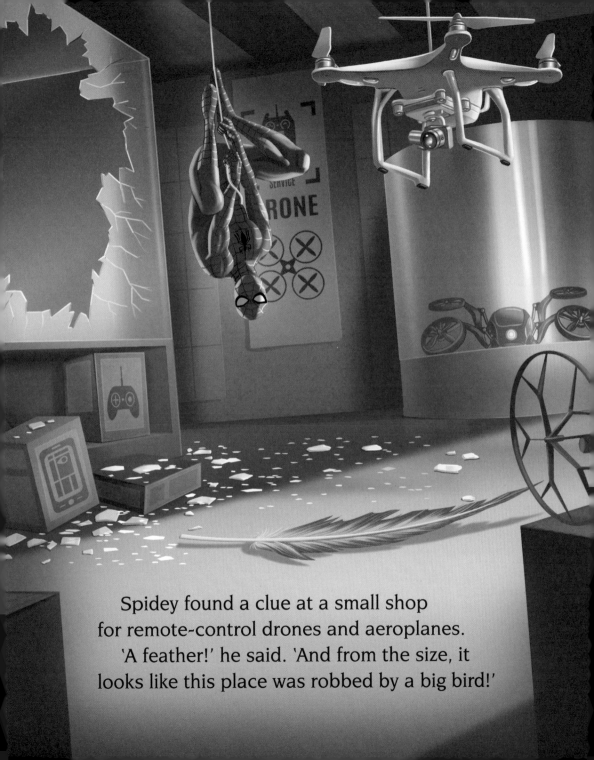

Spidey found a clue at a small shop
for remote-control drones and aeroplanes.
'A feather!' he said. 'And from the size, it
looks like this place was robbed by a big bird!'

Spider-Man found more clues. They led him to Stark Tower. When he landed on the building, his spider-sense started to tingle. Spidey leapt to one side, narrowly avoiding a blast of energy!

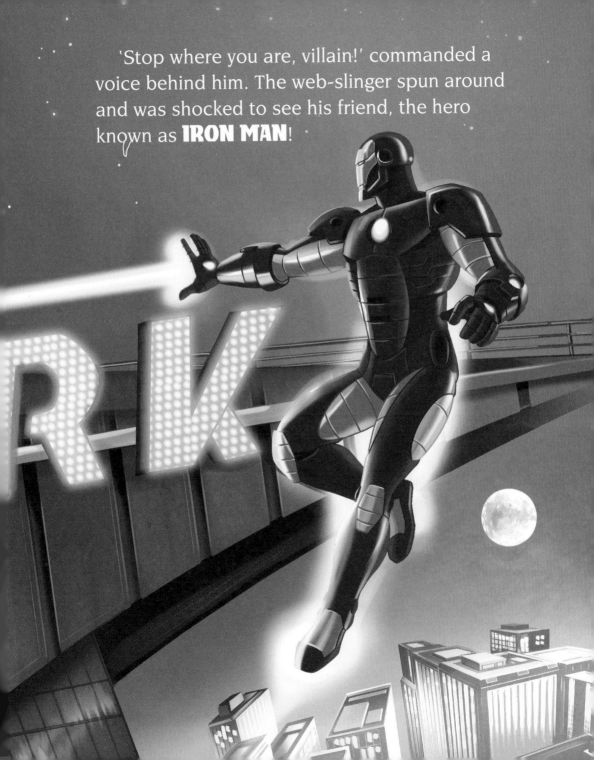

'Stop where you are, villain!' commanded a voice behind him. The web-slinger spun around and was shocked to see his friend, the hero known as **IRON MAN**!

'Apologies, Spider-Man. I thought you were the thief, trying to break into Stark Tower,' said Iron Man.
'No worries, Shellhead,' replied Spidey.
'Is everything safe here?'
'Let's make sure,' Iron Man replied.

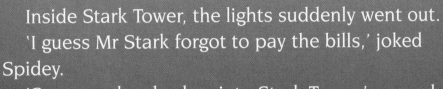

Inside Stark Tower, the lights suddenly went out.

'I guess Mr Stark forgot to pay the bills,' joked Spidey.

'Someone has broken into Stark Tower,' warned Iron Man, 'and I think they're still here!'

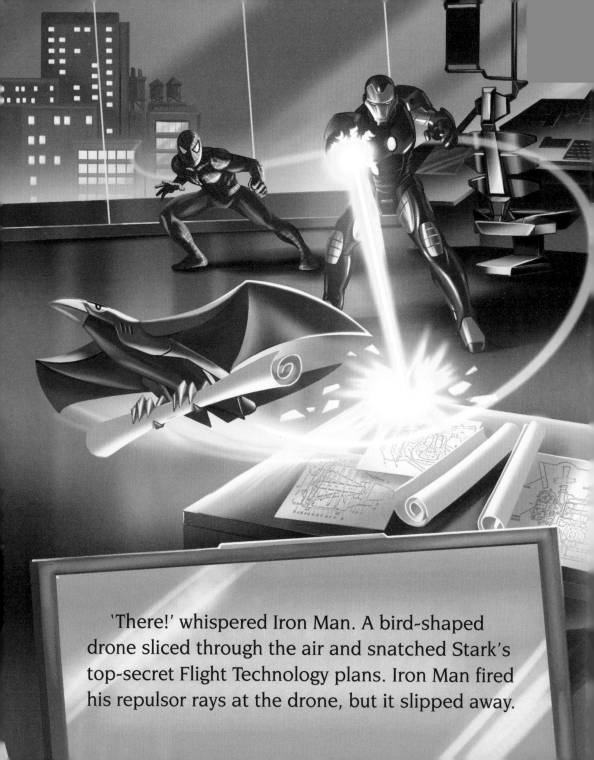

'There!' whispered Iron Man. A bird-shaped drone sliced through the air and snatched Stark's top-secret Flight Technology plans. Iron Man fired his repulsor rays at the drone, but it slipped away.

'Blast that thing, Shellhead!' shouted Spidey
as the drone shot down the hallway. 'Before
it gets out the window!'
   'Too late!' replied Iron Man.

The heroes raced outside and were shocked to discover the villainous **_Vulture_**!
'Now all those tech-shop robberies make sense,' exclaimed Spider-Man. 'He was stealing tech for things that fly.'

'Catch me if you can,
do-gooders!' said the Vulture.
'I have what I came for.'

'Let's get that bad bird,' said Spidey,
'and get your tech plans back!'
'Deal,' replied Iron Man.

The Vulture swooped down and swerved towards the park. He zipped over rocks, around trees and under bridges to escape. But no matter how fast he flew, the villain couldn't get away from the two heroes.

'This will shake you off my tail feathers!'
growled the Vulture, and he filled the air with
more drones to distract the heroes.

'Until next time!' the Vulture cackled,
making his getaway.

'I can't believe the Vulture escaped!' said Iron Man as Spider-Man finished off the last two drones. 'With Stark's new Flight Technology, there's no telling what he'll do next!'

'Cool down, Shellhead! While you were busy blasting drones, I tossed one of my spider-tracers onto our flying foe,' said Spidey. 'Now all we have to do is follow him to his nest.'

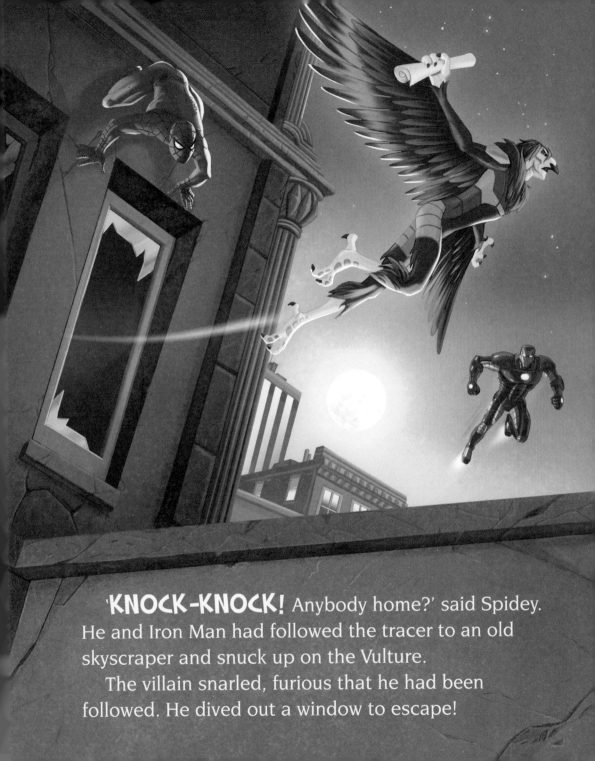

'**KNOCK-KNOCK!** Anybody home?' said Spidey.
He and Iron Man had followed the tracer to an old
skyscraper and snuck up on the Vulture.
    The villain snarled, furious that he had been
followed. He dived out a window to escape!

The Vulture weaved through the city, racing towards a crowded tunnel.
'We can't let him get away again!' shouted Iron Man.

'Don't worry, Shellhead,' Spidey said.
'There's no light at the end of the tunnel
for this flying fugitive!'

Just in the nick of time, Spider-Man covered
the tunnel entrance with webbing – **TWHICK!**
The fast-flying Vulture flew right into it.

'I guess things got a little sticky for the Vulture,'
Iron Man said.

'He'll be back in his cage soon enough!'
Spider-Man replied as he handed the jailbird over
to the police. 'And that's just where he belongs.'

Treasure Cove Stories

Please contact Centum Books to receive the full list of titles in the *Treasure Cove Stories* series.
books@centumbooksltd.co.uk

Classic favourites

1 Three Little Pigs
2 Snow White and the Seven Dwarfs
3 The Fox and the Hound - Hide-and-Seek
4 Dumbo
5 Cinderella
6 Cinderella's Friends
7 Alice in Wonderland
8 Mad Hatter's Tea Party from Alice in Wonderland
9 Mickey Mouse and his Spaceship
10 Peter Pan
11 Pinocchio
12 Mickey and the Beanstalk
13 Sleeping Beauty and the Good Fairies
14 The Lucky Puppy
15 Chicken Little
16 The Incredibles
17 Coco
18 Winnie the Pooh and Tigger
19 The Sword in the Stone
20 Mary Poppins
21 The Jungle Book
22 The Aristocats
23 Lady and the Tramp
24 Bambi
25 Bambi - Friends of the Forest

Recently published

50 Frozen
51 Cinderella is my Babysitter
52 Beauty and the Beast - I am the Beast
53 Blaze and the Monster Machines - Mighty Monster Machines
54 Blaze and the Monster Machines - Dino Parade!
55 Teenage Mutant Ninja Turtles - Follow the Ninja!

56 I am a Princess
57 The Big Book of Paw Patrol
58 Paw Patrol - Adventures with Grandpa!
59 Paw Patrol - Pirate Pups!
60 Trolls
61 Trolls Holiday
62 The Secret Life of Pets
63 Zootropolis
64 Ariel is my Babysitter
65 Tiana is my Babysitter
66 Belle is my Babysitter
67 Paw Patrol - Itty-Bitty Kitty Rescue
68 Moana
69 Nella the Princess Knight - My Heart is Bright!
70 Guardians of the Galaxy
71 Captain America - High-Stakes Heist!
72 Ant-Man
73 The Mighty Avengers
74 The Mighty Avengers - Lights Out!
75 The Incredible Hulk
76 Shimmer & Shine - Wish Upon a Sleepover
77 Shimmer & Shine - Backyard Ballet
78 Paw Patrol - All-Star Pups!
79 Teenage Mutant Ninja Turtles - Really Spaced Out!
80 I am Ariel
81 Madagascar
82 Jasmine is my Babysitter
83 How to Train your Dragon
84 Shrek
85 Puss in Boots
86 Kung Fu Panda
87 Beauty and the Beast - I am Belle
88 The Lion Guard - The Imaginary Okapi
89 Thor - Thunder Strike!
90 Guardians of the Galaxy - Rocket to the Rescue!
91 Nella the Princess Knight - Nella and the Dragon
92 Shimmer & Shine - Treasure Twins!

93 Olaf's Frozen Adventure
94 Black Panther
95 Trolls - Branch's Bunker Birthday
96 Trolls - Poppy's Party
97 The Ugly Duckling
98 Cars - Look Out for Mater!
99 101 Dalmatians
100 The Sorcerer's Apprentice
101 Tangled
102 Avengers - The Threat of Thanos
103 Puppy Dog Pals - Don't Rain on my Pug-Rade
104 Jurassic Park
105 The Mighty Thor
106 Doctor Strange

Latest publications

107 Captain Marvel
108 The Invincible Iron Man
109 Black Panther - Warriors of Wakanda
110 The Big Freeze
111 Ratatouille
112 Aladdin
113 Aladdin - I am the Genie
114 Seven Dwarfs Find a House
115 Toy Story
116 Toy Story 4
117 Paw Patrol - Jurassic Bark!
118 Paw Patrol - Mighty Pup Power!
119 Shimmer & Shine - Pet Talent Show!
120 SpongeBob SquarePants - Krabby Patty Caper
121 The Lion King - I am Simba
122 Winnie the Pooh - The Honey Tree
123 Frozen II
124 Baby Shark and the Colours of the Ocean
125 Baby Shark and the Police Sharks!
126 Trolls World Tour

*Book list may be subject to change.